E is for Election Day

by Gloria M. Gavris   illustrated by Shawn McCann

Checkers
Book Press

Boston • USA

Checkers Book Press, LLC
21 Monadnock Road
Chestnut Hill, MA 02467
www.EisforElectionDay.com
EisforElectionDay@gmail.com

Printed and bound in the United States of America

First Edition

LCCN 2015938231

ISBN 978-0-9962881-0-1 (hc.)   ISBN 978-0-9962881-2-5 (pbk.)

10 9 8 7 6 5 4 3 2 1   10 9 8 7 6 5 4 3 2 1

This book was expertly produced by Book Bridge Press.
www.bookbridgepress.com

Aa is for American Elections

Lucky you! The United States of America has a form of government called a democracy. This means that we can vote for our leaders. These elected officials make the laws that we live by. Voting for our leaders is a great freedom, but with it comes a responsibility to be informed and engaged in our government.

In a democracy, votes influence laws and public policy in the cities, towns, and states where we live. That is pretty powerful!

Bb is for Ballots

Shhhh! A ballot is a piece of paper used to cast a vote. Voters take their ballots into a private voting booth and write down a candidate's name, or mark an X in a box or color a circle next to a candidate's name. After the polls close, all the ballots are counted and then the winner is announced.

Cc is for Conventions

What a party! A political convention is a big, fun event with lots of people, signs, balloons, and speeches. There are two separate conventions, one for the Democrats and one for the Republicans. At a convention, the candidates running for office are nominated by people called delegates, who represent cities, towns, or states. The two candidates chosen at the convention then run against

Dd is for Debates

Debates are public discussions that help people decide who to vote for. All the candidates get together and answer questions asked by a moderator. People often watch debates on TV or the Internet, or listen to them on the radio. Debates help voters decide who they like, depending on the candidates' answers. During one presidential debate, someone asked the presidential candidates what kind of underwear they wore, boxers or briefs! Isn't that a silly question? Most questions and issues are more serious than that. They concern taxes, education, and public safety. What question would you ask a candidate running for office?

Ee is for Election Day

Election Day is the day every campaign works hard to prepare for. On this day voters go to the polls and cast their ballots. Votes are counted and a winner is announced. Polls are typically open from 7:00 AM to 8:00 PM so that people have all the time they need to get to the polls and vote. Election Day is usually the first Tuesday in November.

Ff is for Fundraising

When you run for political office you need money to pay for bumper stickers, lawn signs, advertising, balloons, a website, a campaign office, and many more things that make a campaign successful. Fundraising is very important to political campaigns to help candidates get their messages to voters. To raise money, campaigns have parties, send out requests in the mail, or solicit funds through their websites on the Internet. Every little bit helps.

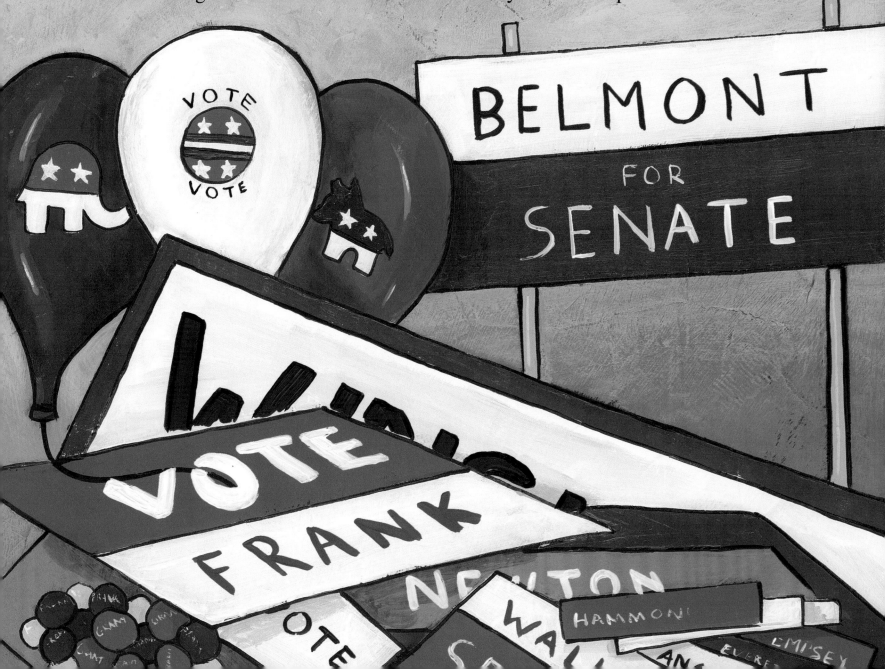

Gg is for Grassroots Efforts

Anyone running for mayor, city council, or president needs volunteers. Candidates start with their friends and neighbors to build support for their campaign. Little by little, supporters and campaign organizations grow and grow. This is called building a "grassroots" effort. The candidate tells a friend, who tells a friend, who tells a friend, who tells a friend, and so on.

Hh is for Handshakes

"How are you doing?" "Nice to meet you!" Candidates love to shake hands, say hello, and greet folks with a smile. When a candidate is running for office, he or she needs to meet lots of people and try to win their votes. Candidates will shake hundreds of hands during a campaign. Do you have a firm handshake? You will need one if you want to run for office!

Ii is for Internet

Computers and mobile phones can elect a candidate? Yes, they can! The Internet has changed the way candidates reach voters. Candidates can announce they are running for office with an online video, or the campaign can have a social media site where they post pictures and information about campaign events. The Internet has helped candidates reach thousands of voters. But if you want to be elected, be careful no one posts a silly picture of you online. It could hurt your reputation and campaign!

Jj is for Judge for Yourself

Who will I vote for? It can be so hard to make decisions between candidates sometimes. Your family and friends may not all agree with your choice, so it is up to you! That is why you need lots of information to make a good decision. Visit candidates' websites to read about the issues they think are important. Watch a debate. Listen to commercials. Read the newspaper. You are going to have to judge for yourself which candidate is trustworthy and also shares your interests and values.

Kk is for Kids

Candidates need many volunteers to help run a great campaign. You can help by folding letters, knocking on doors, blowing up balloons, making phone calls, and holding signs. To run for office, candidates need help from many different kinds of people. Kids, college students, grown-ups, and grandparents all can volunteer. How would you try to help a candidate win an election?

Ll is for **Legal Age to Vote**

On July 1, 1971, the 26th Amendment to the U.S. Constitution was ratified, or passed, granting the right to vote to anyone eighteen years old or older. After a citizen turns eighteen, he or she can go to the local city hall or town hall and register to vote. How many more years will it be before you can vote?

Mm is for Major Political Parties

A political party is a group of people who hold similar beliefs on taxation, states' rights, national defense, and government spending. In the United States there are many political parties. The two most popular are the Republicans and the Democrats. In 1874, Thomas Nast, a political cartoonist, drew a donkey dressed in a lion's suit scaring away the forest animals. The elephant was labeled "The Republican Vote." This popular cartoon is why the Democrats' symbol became the donkey and the Republicans' symbol became the elephant.

Nn is for Nomination Papers

Filing nomination papers is among the first steps in running for political office. Candidates stand in front of post offices and supermarkets and go door to door asking voters to show their support by writing their signature on nomination petitions. If a candidate gets enough signatures, his or her nomination papers are delivered to the town or city hall to be certified. The candidate's name is then approved to be placed on the ballot. Let the campaigning begin!

Oo is for Oath of Office

Once a candidate is elected, he or she must take an oath of office. This is a promise an elected official makes to the voters. You should practice this oath of office. You might be president of the United States someday!

"I do solemnly swear that I will faithfully execute the office of President of the United States, and will to the best of my ability, preserve, protect, and defend the Constitution of the United States."

Pp is for Primary Day

A preliminary election is held if more than one person from the same political party is running for the same office. This event is called "primary day." The winner on primary day will represent his or her political party on Election Day. The campaign isn't over yet. There is still more campaigning to do before Election Day!

Qq is for Qualifications

Can anyone run for president? In order to run for president of the United States, a person must have been born in the United States, must be at least thirty-five years old, and must have been a resident of the United States for more than fourteen years. That's it! It could be you someday!

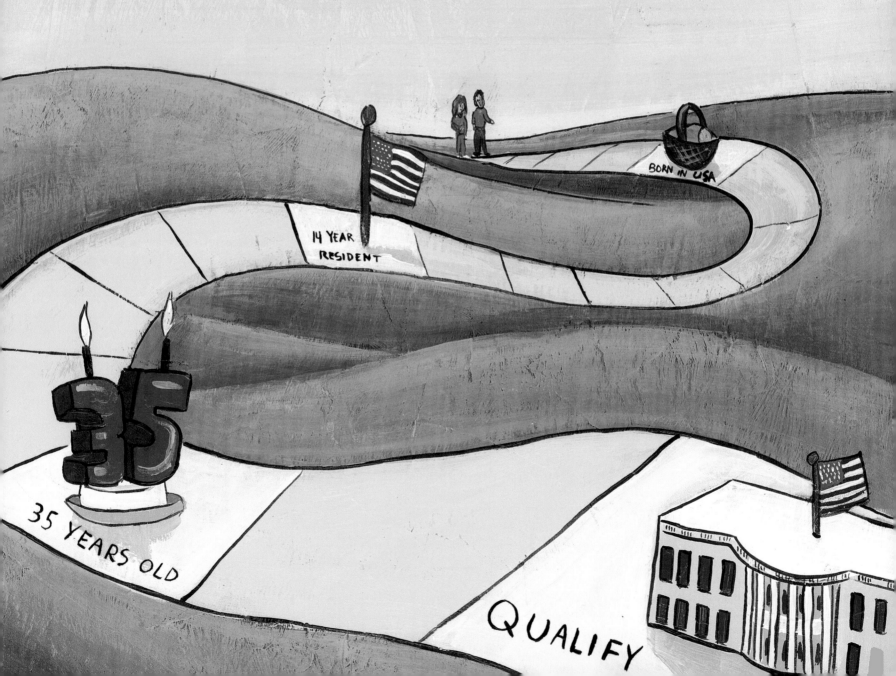

Rr is for Recount

What happens if someone works really hard to win an election and the vote is very close? When this happens the candidate can ask for a recount. What do you think happens in a recount? Yes, that's right! *All* the votes are counted again to make sure there were no mistakes in the original count and the declared winner is really the winner.

Ss is for Sign Holding

Have you ever seen people waving and holding signs with names on them in September, October, or November? It's probably campaign season! Candidates and their volunteers are trying to get voters to remember their names so they will vote for them. Candidates work very hard trying to win votes, even standing out in the rain and cold! When you walk or drive by, wave or honk your horn to show support! Show the candidate and volunteers that you appreciate how hard they are working.

Tt is for Term Limits

Term limits define how long a candidate can remain in an elected position. The president of the United States can serve for only eight years, or can be elected only twice; each presidential term is four years. But members of Congress—senators and representatives—can be reelected over and over again! There are no term limits for members of Congress. Do you think there should be a limit on how many years someone can serve?

Uu is for Uncle Sam

In 1812 a businessman from Massachusetts named Samuel Wilson moved to Troy, New York. He supplied meat to the U.S. Army and stamped the barrels "U.S." When asked what the initials stood for, one of Wilson's workers said, "Uncle Sam Wilson." New Yorkers began to associate the "U.S." stamped on the barrels with "Uncle Sam." This local saying became a national legend.

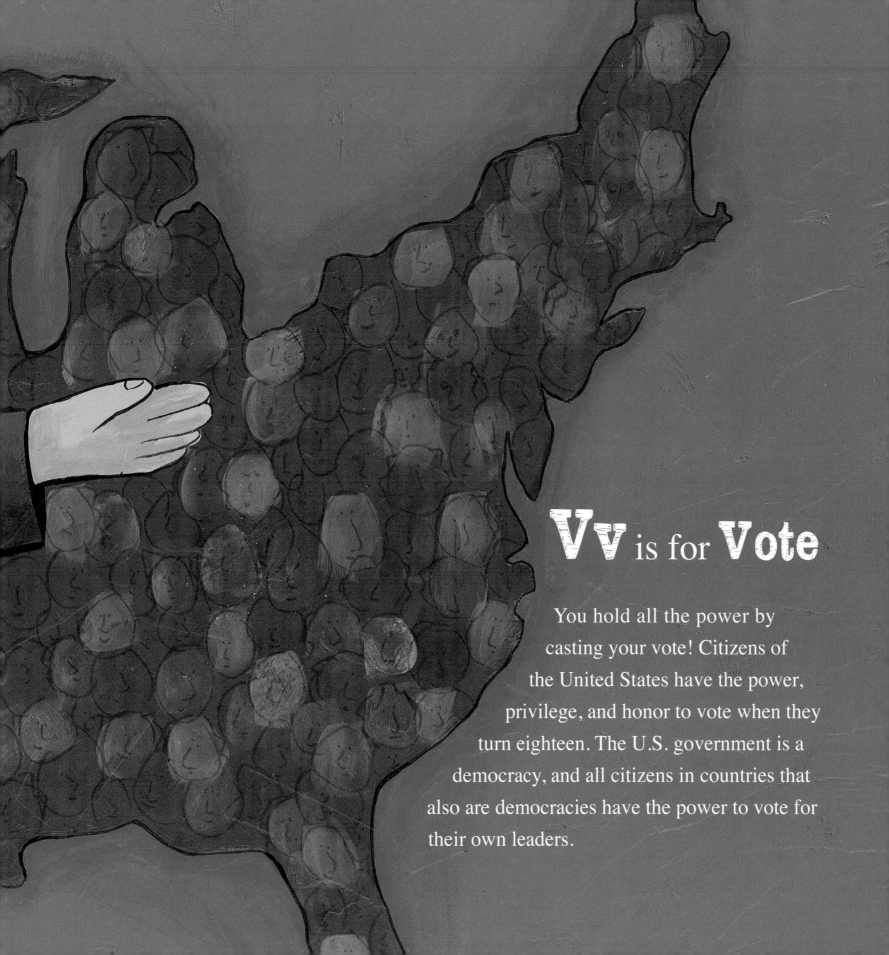

Vv is for Vote

You hold all the power by casting your vote! Citizens of the United States have the power, privilege, and honor to vote when they turn eighteen. The U.S. government is a democracy, and all citizens in countries that also are democracies have the power to vote for their own leaders.

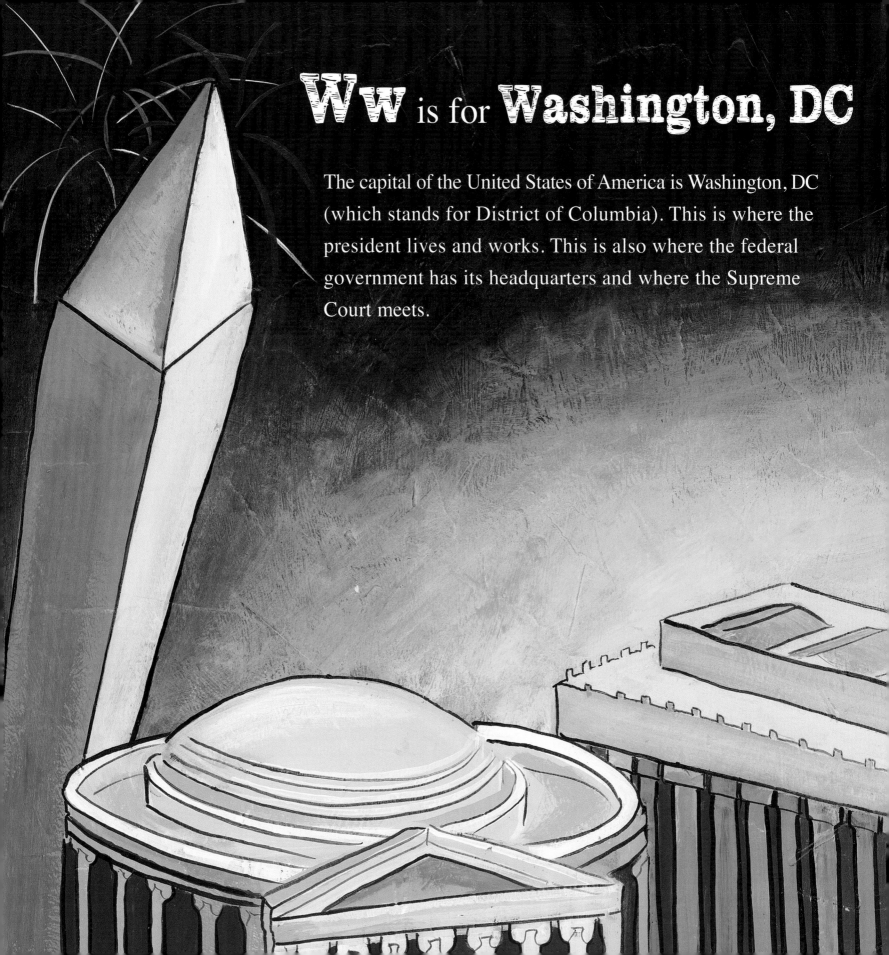

Ww is for Washington, DC

The capital of the United States of America is Washington, DC (which stands for District of Columbia). This is where the president lives and works. This is also where the federal government has its headquarters and where the Supreme Court meets.

The city was named to honor George Washington, America's first president. Washington, DC, is filled with important history and has many monuments and museums. Have you visited Washington, DC? Maybe you will someday. It is fun and you might even get to see the president!

EXIT POLL SENATE

62% BELMONT

38% EVERETT

Xx is for eXit Polls

Exit polls are questions voters are asked immediately after they have finished voting and have left their polling location. An exit poll often asks voters which candidate they voted for. On election night, exit polls are helpful to candidates and the media to help them predict who the actual winner will be before the votes have been counted and certified.

Yy is for You

This is the most important letter in our book! Always remember how important *you* are to the electoral process. You can make a real difference in your government. Learn about issues and candidates. When an issue is important to you, there are many ways you can make a difference, such as volunteering your time or voting for your favorite candidate. You might even decide to run for office someday. Remember, *you* make democracy happen!

Zz is for Zig Zag

Candidates need comfortable shoes
because they will be zigzagging
through neighborhoods! In order
to win elections, candidates spend
time knocking on doors, introducing
themselves to voters, and
talking about the issues
that concern people.
I hope you zigzag
your way to
victory and win
an election
someday!